G. P. Putnam's Sons, a division of
Penguin Putnam Books for Young Readers,
345 Hudson Street, New York, NY 10014.
G. P. Putnam's Sons, Reg. U.S. Pat. & Tm. Off.
Published simultaneously in Canada. Printed in
Hong Kong by South China Printing Co. (1988) Ltd.
Designed by Gunta Alexander. Text set in Apollo.
The art was done in pastels.
Library of Congress Cataloging-in-Publication Data
Isadora, Rachel. Peekaboo morning / Rachel Isadora.
p. cm.   Summary: A toddler plays peekaboo
throughout the day. [1. Toddlers—Fiction.
2. African Americans—Fiction.]
I. Title. PZ7.I1763 Pe 2001
[E]—dc21 2001016245
ISBN 0-399-23602-3
10 9 8 7 6 5 4 3 2 1
First Impression

Peekaboo Morning

RACHEL ISADORA

G. P. PUTNAM'S SONS · NEW YORK

Peekaboo! I see...

my mommy

Peekaboo! I see...

my daddy

Peekaboo! I see...

me

Peekaboo! I see...

my puppy

Peekaboo! I see...

my train

Peekaboo! I see...

my grandma

Peekaboo! I see…

my
grandpa

Peekaboo! I see...

a bunny

Peekaboo! I see...

a butterfly

Peekaboo! I see...

my friend

Peekaboo! I see…

you!